INTERRUPTING COW

Meets the
Wise Quacker

To Adam and Betsy, definitely wise quackers
—J. Y.

To Dalia and Melina, two funny little ducks
—J. D.

SIMON SPOTLIGHT
An imprint of Simon & Schuster Children's Publishing Division
1230 Avenue of the Americas, New York, New York 10020
This Simon Spotlight edition May 2024
Text copyright © 2024 by Jane Yolen
Illustrations copyright © 2024 by Joëlle Dreidemy
Simon & Schuster: Celebrating 100 Years of Publishing in 2024
For information about special discounts for bulk purchases, please contact
Simon & Schuster Special Sales at 1-866-506-1949 or business@simonandschuster.com.
The Simon & Schuster Speakers Bureau can bring authors to your live event. For more information or to
book an event contact the Simon & Schuster Speakers Bureau at 1-866-248-3049 or visit our website at
www.simonspeakers.com.
Manufactured in the United States of America 0324 LAK
10 9 8 7 6 5 4 3 2 1
Library of Congress Cataloging-in-Publication Data
Names: Yolen, Jane, author. | Dreidemy, Joëlle, illustrator.
Title: Interrupting Cow meets the Wise Quacker / by Jane Yolen; illustrated by Joëlle Dreidemy.
Description: Simon Spotlight edition. | New York : Simon Spotlight, 2024. |
Series: Interrupting Cow | Audience: Ages 5 to 7. | Summary: Interrupting Cow meets a duck who knows
more jokes than anyone on the farm.
Identifiers: LCCN 2023029914 (print) | LCCN 2023029915 (ebook) | ISBN 9781665932745 (paperback) |
ISBN 9781665932752 (hardcover) | ISBN 9781665932769 (ebook)
Subjects: CYAC: Jokes—Fiction. | Cows—Fiction. | Ducks—Fiction. | Domestic animals—Fiction. |
Friendship—Fiction. | Humorous stories. |LCGFT: Animal fiction. | Humorous fiction. |
Picture books. | Readers (Publications) Classification: LCC PZ7.Y78 Im 2024 (print) | LCC PZ7.Y78
(ebook) | DDC [E]—dc23
LC record available at https://lccn.loc.gov/2023029914
LC ebook record available at https://lccn.loc.gov/2023029915

InterRupting COW

Meets the
Wise QuackeR

by Jane Yolen
illustrated by Joëlle Dreidemy

Ready-to-Read

Simon Spotlight
New York London Toronto Sydney New Delhi

It was another morning on the farm. Interrupting Cow woke with a head full of jokes she had learned from some new friends but no one to tell them to.

The herd disliked jokes.
The horses, goats, and pigs all hid
when they saw her coming.

But Interrupting Cow was an
op-ti-mist—
a cow who always hoped for the best.
Maybe today will be different,
she thought.
So she said, "Knock, knock . . ."

But without waiting for her
to say one word more,
all the animals headed
for the barn door
and did not stop to open it,
just ran right through it,
knocking it to the ground.

For a moment, Interrupting Cow
thought she was having a bad dream.
But when she went to the door,
it was indeed lying on the ground,
with dozens of hoofprints covering it.
Interrupting Cow stepped outside,
careful to avoid any splinters.

On the other side stood a large duck, sort of yellow, as if he had never quite outgrown his duckling feathers. He was chuckling at the door disaster. "You are not one of our ducks," Interrupting Cow said. "You are far too yellow, and you know how to laugh."

The duck nodded and gave her
a wide grin. "I come from a long line
of wise quackers," he said.
"We love to collect jokes."

"I love knocks-knocks especially,"
said the duck, standing with his wings
on hips, waiting.
Interrupting Cow was delighted.

"Knock, knock," she began.
"Who's there?" he asked.
"Interrupting Cow!" she cried out.

"Interrupting Cow—" the duck began, his gleaming eyes showing that he knew what was coming.

But before he could finish saying
"Interrupting Cow who?"
she interrupted, shouting: "MOO!"

Cow and duck fell down in giggles
that mixed moos and quacks
and went on and on and on and on.

Still chuckling, the pair got up.
They wandered off while the sound
of the farmer's hammer fixing the door
followed them down the road.

"Do you know any other cow jokes?"
asked the duck. "Remember, I
collect jokes."

"A few," said Interrupting Cow, "but
not enough. If you teach me others,
maybe then the herd will like me."

"Unlikely," said Wise Quacker. "I have found very few cows with a sense of humor."

"Try me!" Interrupting Cow pleaded.

They had reached the duck pond.
The paddling ducks took one look
at them and swam away so fast,
they left a tiny tidal wave behind.
Nearby goats climbed onto their
houses and baaed loudly to keep out
the sound of any jokes.

Pigs sank deep into the mud
that filled their ears,
so they could not hear.
And the horses all galloped away
to the far side of the meadow,
to mix in with the herd of cows.

Wise Quacker reached deep under his wing and came up with a little book. When he opened it, Interrupting Cow saw that it was filled with scratches and hatches. He began to read: "What did one secret agent cow say to the other?
Are you **udder cover**?"

"I love that," Interrupting Cow
interrupted. "Do you know this one?
Why was the cow sad?
She wasn't sad, just **moo-dy**."
Wise Quacker laughed.
Then he read another joke,
his beak buried in his book.

"You know what they say about
cows . . .
they're **outstanding in their field**."
Interrupting Cow laughed.

Wise Quacker turned a few pages and continued:

"What do cows play in bands?

Moo-sic!

What do you get if you pamper a cow?

Spoiled milk.

What do cows read in the morning?
The **moos-paper**.
What does the farmer say
to the cows at night?
It's **pasture bedtime**."

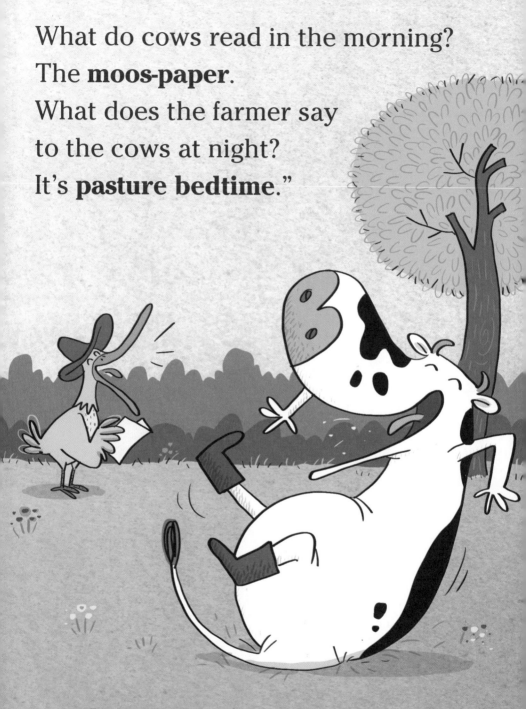

Interrupting Cow laughed
and laughed and laughed.

Then it was Interrupting Cow's turn.
"Here's my last one," she said,
and took a deep breath.
"Why do cows have bells?
Because **their horns don't work.**"

Wise Quacker quickly scribbled that joke in his book, then put it back under his wing. "And here's *my* last one." He took a deep breath. "Knock, knock."

"Who's there?" asked Interrupting Cow.
"Interrupting Cow," he said.
"Interrupting Cow wh—"
"MOO!" Wise Quacker and Interrupting Cow yelled together.

Then they began to laugh,
stomping hoof and wing.
"Still the best cow joke of them all,"
said Interrupting Cow.
"Absolutely!" said Wise Quacker.
"Listening to new jokes today
was a *moooving* experience,"
Interrupting Cow said.
They both fell to the ground again.
They were laughing so hard that
Interrupting Cow said, "This time,
I might have spoiled the milk."

She closed her eyes for a moment
and suddenly heard bubbles of laughter.
When she opened her eyes,
she saw that every one of her
animal friends was clapping and hooting
and howling with laughter.

A great ending, Interrupting Cow thought.
But whatever can I do for an encore?